PUFFIN BOOKS

UK | USA | Canada | Ireland | Australia | India | New Zealand | South Africa

Puffin Books is part of the Penguin Random House group of companies
whose addresses can be found at global.penguinrandomhouse.com.

www.penguin.co.uk   www.puffin.co.uk   www.ladybird.co.uk

Penguin
Random House
UK

First published 2016
001

Printed in China
A CIP catalogue record for this book is available from the British Library

HB: 978-0-141-36786-6
PB: 978-0-141-36787-3

All correspondence to:
Puffin Books, Penguin Random House Children's
80 Strand, London WC2R 0RL

A tale of Moominvalley

MOOMIN
and the
Ocean's Song

BASED ON THE ORIGINAL STORIES BY

Tove Jansson

PUFFIN

Moomintroll was having a mending morning, repairing the mast on the little bark schooner his mother had made for him.

"Pee-hoo!" whistled Moomin cheerfully as he admired his handiwork. "She'll sail beautifully now!"

Little My had been keeping Moomin company –
secretly hoping to get her hands on the glue pot.
Her eyes lit up at the sound of a loud crash.

"What was that?" cried Moomintroll.
"A catastrophe!" Little My grinned
and scampered off to investigate.

It turned out to be Moominpappa.
While searching for his easel in the attic,
he had knocked over a great stack of clutter.

He was staring at one of the toppled boxes.
"Bless my tail!" he said.
"My old Discovery Collection!"

Moominpappa began rooting about in the box. He took out a splendid seashell, held it to one ear and gave a happy sigh.

"Ah, the Song of the Ocean! Still as clear as day, after all these years!"

Moominmamma had heard the crash too and came hurrying up the attic steps.

Little My had her ear pressed to Moominpappa's seashell. "Hmph!" she snorted. "I can't hear any silly old song!"

"Of course not, my dear," said Moominmamma, relieved to find everyone unhurt. "Only a shell's finder can hear its song. Now, come along, children. Let's give Pappa some time alone with his collection."

Later that morning, Moomintroll told Snorkmaiden about the shell as they took a stroll together. "The Ocean's Song?" gasped Snorkmaiden. "How exciting! I wish I could hear it too."

Seeing her delight, Moomin was struck by a bold idea.

"We could look for our own singing shells," he said.
Snorkmaiden clasped her hands.
"Oh, yes! Let's!"

"We'll talk to Snufkin," said Moomin.
"He'll know the proper way to go about it."

Sure enough, Snufkin had an idea of where to look. "Lonely Island," he told Moomin. "That could be a place for shells. There's all sorts of magic there."

Sniff pulled a face. "But that's far out at sea!" he squeaked.

"Any discovery worth making starts with a sea voyage," said Snufkin wisely.

"A discovery?" Sniff perked up.

"You mean like . . . treasure?"

And so it was that, just before noon,
the four friends set sail in the *Moominfamily's*
little boat, the *Adventure*. Before long, she was
skimming over the open ocean.

"Land ahoy!" squealed Sniff with some relief.
"Lonely Island," said Snufkin, peering ahead.
"Right where it should be."

As they drew closer to the island's shore, Snorkmaiden's eyes widened. "Oh!" she gasped. "Look!"

Two beautiful silver-maned creatures were frisking in the shallow water.

"Seahorses!" cried Moomin.

A moment later the shy creatures had spotted them – and vanished below the waves.

Together, the friends hauled the *Adventure*
up on to the shore.
"Treasure-hunt time!" squeaked Sniff.

There were certainly all sorts of seashells.
Moomintroll, keen to impress Snorkmaiden,
set about finding one like Moominpappa's.

But it was no use. Moomin tried shell after
shell, but none held the Ocean's Song. Only
one made any noise at all – a faint tinkling
when he shook it.

Then a whistle from Snufkin made
Moomin abandon his search.

A fleet of tiny boats was sailing towards Lonely Island. They were crammed with small, thin ghost-white figures.

"Hattifatteners," said Snufkin.

Keeping out of sight, the friends watched the fleet approach.

"There must be hundreds of them!" whispered Snorkmaiden.

The first boats landed. Their pale passengers glided silently ashore. Before long, the beach was crowded with Hattifatteners, glowing faintly as they swayed.

The Hattifatteners began to drift away, without a sound, towards the centre of the island.

Snufkin frowned. "They only get together like this for one reason," he told Moomin. "To recharge. In a lightning storm."

They looked up at a sky rapidly darkening with grey cloud.

"Ooooo!" squealed Sniff, terrified. "I knew a sea trip spelled trouble!"

"We should have checked Moominpappa's barometer this morning," whispered Snorkmaiden, a little afraid.

Moomin was fascinated by the Hattifatteners, and he still hadn't found the Ocean's Song. But, when he saw Sniff quivering with fright, he knew he had to help his friends get home.

Moomin would never forget the homeward voyage. They tried to race the storm, but it easily overtook them. Lightning flickered, the rain lashed down and the *Adventure* was tossed about by the churning sea.

"We'll all be drowned!" wailed Sniff, clinging to the mast. "Twice over!"

It was a very wet, very bedraggled crew who reached the Moominvalley landing stage at last as the storm finally moved on. They were all happy to be home.

Once back at the Moominhouse, Moominmamma admired their island finds.

"What lovely shells, my dears!"

Moomin could not help wishing that one, at least, held the Ocean's Song. A little sadly, he gave his own shell a shake to make it tinkle . . .

. . . and something small and silvery fell out on to the table.

"That's a seahorse-shoe!" cried Moominpappa. "Very rare – and a powerful good-luck charm!"

Moominmamma found a spare hatbox of Moominpappa's in which to keep the little seahorse-shoe safe.

"It can be the start of your own Discovery Collection!" said Snorkmaiden.

Moomin felt very happy indeed, and so proud that he and his friends had brought home such a rare treasure. He was quite sure that with its good luck to share they would make many more exciting discoveries together in the long summer days to come.

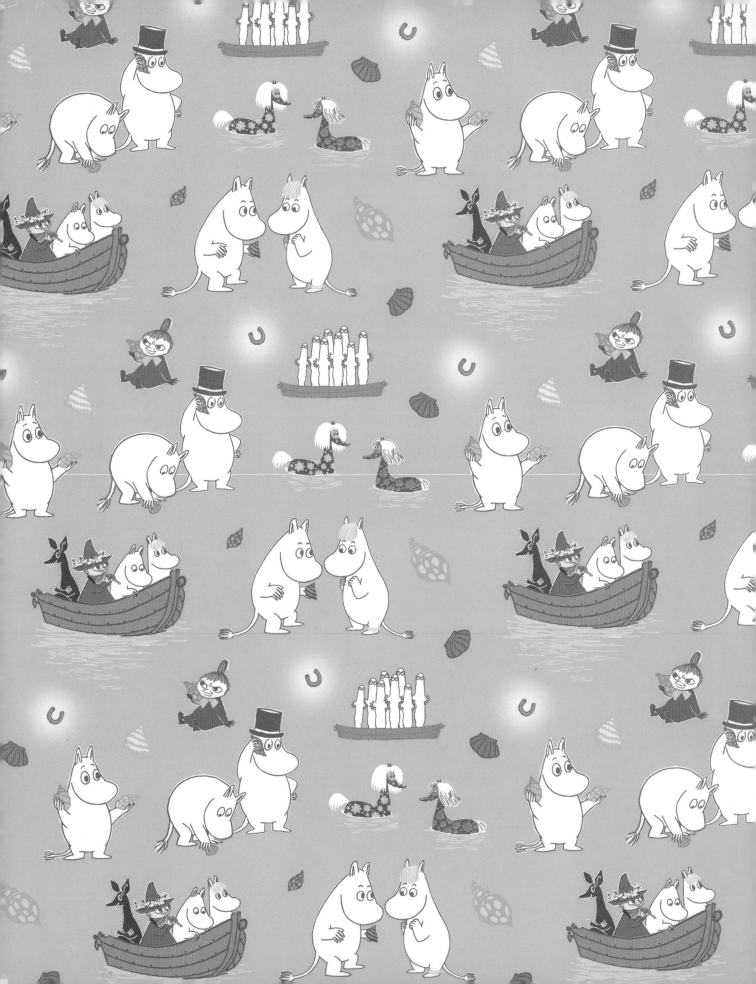